SEA SERPENT

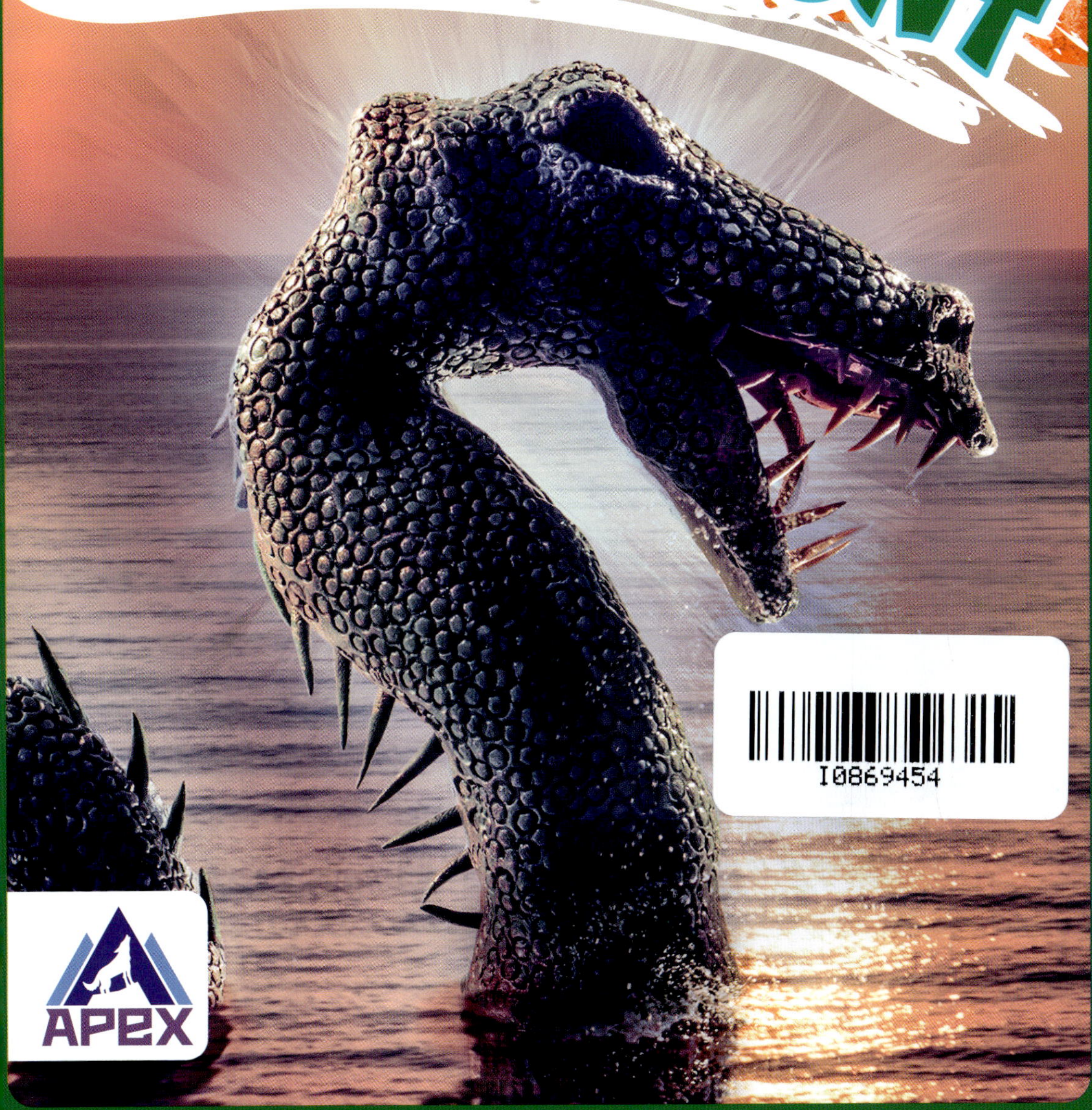

APEX

By Christine Ha

WWW.APEXEDITIONS.COM

Apex is distributed by North Star Editions:
sales@northstareditions.com | 888-417-0195

Produced for Apex by Red Line Editorial.

Photographs ©: Shutterstock Images, cover, 1, 4–5, 6–7, 12, 13, 14–15, 18–19, 20, 22–23, 26–27, 29; North Wind Picture Archives/AP Images, 8; iStockphoto, 9, 10–11, 16–17, 21, 24–25

Library of Congress Control Number: 2020952950

ISBN
978-1-63738-024-6 (hardcover)
978-1-63738-060-4 (paperback)
978-1-63738-129-8 (ebook pdf)
978-1-63738-096-3 (hosted ebook)

Printed in the United States of America
Mankato, MN
082021

NOTE TO PARENTS AND EDUCATORS

Apex books are designed to build literacy skills in striving readers. Exciting, high-interest content attracts and holds readers' attention. The text is carefully leveled to allow students to achieve success quickly. Additional features, such as bolded glossary words for difficult terms, help build comprehension.

TABLE OF CONTENTS

CHAPTER 1

A NARROW ESCAPE

The sailors hear a loud boom. Then their ship rocks to one side. A sea serpent is attacking!

A sea serpent's body can be much longer than a ship.

Sea serpents are said to be fast, powerful swimmers.

The captain spins the ship's wheel. But he can't turn fast enough. The sea serpent strikes again. Huge waves splash onto the deck. Soon, the ship will sink.

Some sea serpents wrap their bodies around ships to sink them.

But the crew is in luck. A gust of wind blows. It fills the sails. The ship races away. For now, the crew is safe.

Sea serpents have long, thin bodies. A few have wings or legs.

Sea serpents and other monsters decorate an old map of northern Europe.

MONSTER MAPS

In the past, sailors told stories about monsters at sea. Artists drew some of these creatures on maps. Some people made journeys to see if the monsters were real.

CHAPTER 2

MONSTERS OF THE SEA

Many **cultures** tell stories of sea monsters. These creatures often look like huge snakes or dragons.

Tales of sea serpents are hundreds of years old.

Some tales come from Europe. These stories began in **Scandinavia**. Sailors told of terrifying monsters. They said the beasts sank ships.

The Vikings of Scandinavia were skilled sailors. They sailed boats called longships.

The Vikings decorated their boats with carvings of dragons or other creatures.

One story tells of a huge sea serpent. It could wrap around the whole world.

Other stories come from Asia. For example, Japanese **folklore** tells of a mighty dragon. He is the god of the sea. He has great power. He controls the **tides**.

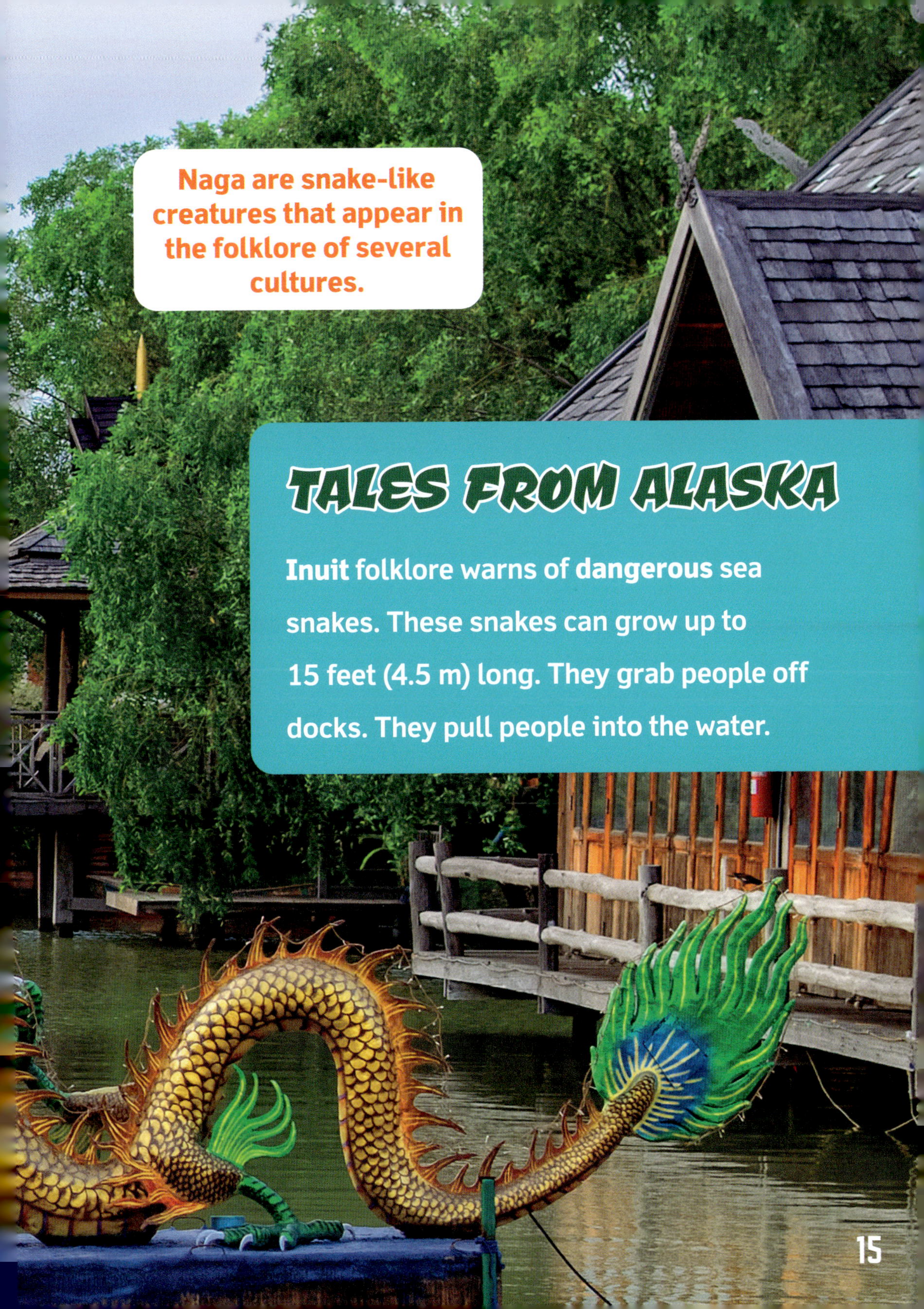

Naga are snake-like creatures that appear in the folklore of several cultures.

TALES FROM ALASKA

Inuit folklore warns of **dangerous** sea snakes. These snakes can grow up to 15 feet (4.5 m) long. They grab people off docks. They pull people into the water.

CHAPTER 3

SHIP SINKER

In the 1500s, a Swedish writer made books and maps. They told about Scandinavia. Some had stories and drawings of sea serpents.

Old illustrations often show sea monsters chasing ships.

Many sea serpents have sharp teeth and spikes on their backs.

The writer said sea serpents were huge. They could grow 200 feet (61 m) long. They had black scales and bright red eyes. They were dangerous, too. At night, they hunted for food.

Some sea serpents are shown with manes like lions.

Sometimes, sea serpents ate animals. Other times, they attacked ships and ate sailors.

Canadian folklore tells of a monster that lives in Okanagan Lake.

Loch Ness is a lake in Scotland. Legend says a monster lives in its waters.

LAKE MONSTER

Stories say a large monster **lurks** in Loch Ness. Most people think it is just a **legend**. But some people travel to the lake. They try to see the monster.

CHAPTER 4

REAL-LIFE CREATURES

Some snakes live in warm ocean waters. But legends say sea serpents live in cold places. So, scientists think sea serpents may be based on other animals.

Sea snakes live in the warm waters of the Indian and Pacific Oceans.

Oarfish are harmless to humans. They eat fish and tiny sea creatures.

For example, people may have seen oarfish. These fish are long and flat. They usually swim deep underwater. But sometimes they come near the surface.

Oarfish can grow up to 36 feet (11 m) long.

Basking sharks often swim near the surface with their mouths open.

Basking sharks can grow 40 feet (12 m) long.

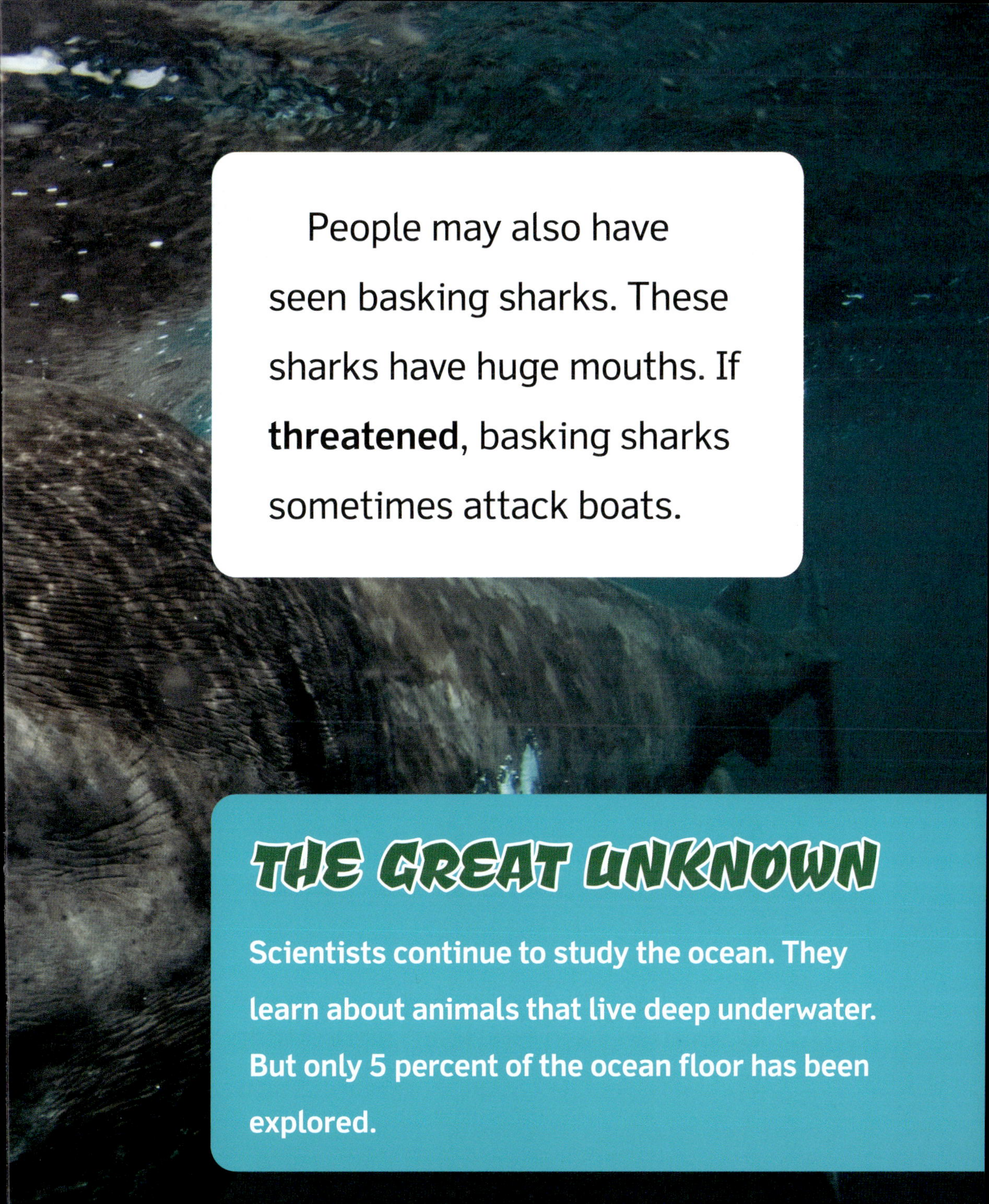

People may also have seen basking sharks. These sharks have huge mouths. If **threatened**, basking sharks sometimes attack boats.

THE GREAT UNKNOWN

Scientists continue to study the ocean. They learn about animals that live deep underwater. But only 5 percent of the ocean floor has been explored.

COMPREHENSION QUESTIONS

Write your answers on a separate piece of paper.

1. Write a few sentences describing the main ideas of Chapter 4.

2. Would you want to visit places where legends said sea serpents lived? Why or why not?

3. Which stories tell of sea serpents that pull people off docks and into the water?

- **A.** Inuit folklore
- **B.** Japanese folklore
- **C.** Scandinavian folklore

4. Why might people who saw oarfish think the animals were sea serpents?

- **A.** Oarfish have long, snake-like bodies.
- **B.** Oarfish have big mouths and sharp teeth.
- **C.** Oarfish often attack and sink ships.

5. What does **beasts** mean in this book?

*Sailors told of terrifying monsters. They said the **beasts** sank ships.*

A. small birds
B. safe places
C. dangerous animals

6. What does **gust** mean in this book?

*A **gust** of wind blows. It fills the sails.*

A. a time of no light
B. a very soft sound
C. a strong rush of air

Answer key on page 32.

GLOSSARY

cultures
Groups of people and the ways they live, including their beliefs and laws.

dangerous
Likely to cause problems or harm.

folklore
Traditional stories common to a group of people.

Inuit
People who are native to cold, northern parts of Canada, Alaska, and Greenland.

legend
A famous story, often based on facts but not always completely true.

lurks
Hides and waits, often in order to surprise or attack.

Scandinavia
An area in northern Europe that includes the countries of Norway, Sweden, Denmark, Iceland, and Finland.

threatened
Put in danger.

tides
The rise and fall of water on the seashore at different times of day.

TO LEARN MORE

BOOKS

Abdo, Kenny. *Cryptids*. Minneapolis: Abdo Publishing, 2020.

Goddu, Krystyna Poray. *Sea Monsters: From Kraken to Nessie*. Minneapolis: Lerner Publications, 2017.

Owings, Lisa. *Ghosts at Sea*. Minneapolis: Bellwether Media, 2017.

ONLINE RESOURCES

Visit **www.apexeditions.com** to find links and resources related to this title.

ABOUT THE AUTHOR

Christine Ha lives in Minnesota. Her search for the Loch Ness Monster was not successful. But she still stares into bodies of water, hoping to see a sea monster lurking in their depths.

INDEX

Answer Key:
1. Answers will vary; **2.** Answers will vary; **3.** A; **4.** A; **5.** C; **6.** C